LONDON CALLING

Bill McKnight

John,

    May you enjoy this short story. It only took 61 years to brew!

      Blessings,

        Bill (2019)

Paperback Edition August 29, 2019
ISBN 9781087237961
© Bill McKnight. All rights reserved.

Bill McKnight lives in North Belfast. He was educated at Cliftonville Primary School and Belfast Royal Academy. He is a member of Ballysillan Presbyterian Church. His hobbies include writing and fly-fishing.

To Stanley McDowell

Foreword

Is Psychiatry necessary? More and more people are becoming mentally unwell. How might we be helped? Is financial investment in community care and periods of in-stay hospitalization key to stabilization, recovery and wellness?

The pain of mental illness is excruciating (as everyone who has experienced such suffering knows). Psychiatric medication does help ease our pain. However, service users can relapse time and time again in spite of taking medication.

It seems to the author that medication deals with symptoms. Insight deals with causes. If we cannot see 'why' we are mentally ill there remains a great need for Psychiatry and psychiatric medication. In our fears and panic and pain Psychiatry has a vital role. But we must look beyond Psychiatry. Perhaps this can only happen when we realise our greatest need?

Introduction

Telling stories is as old as humankind. Telling stories is one way of enabling us to understand the world we live in. We know and we are known. Good stories brim with life making sense.

Bill McKnight's story reflects a search for meaning beyond madness; of hope beyond appearance. Bill's trademark wit, winsomeness, unflinching honesty and what holy books call 'Grace,' jumps off the page and into the reader's heart.

To spend a brief time with Bill in his story brings you into a world which you may never have known or experienced but your heart will no doubt be richer for having spent time within it.

Rev. Reuben McCormick

"Go round and ask all your neighbours for empty jars. Don't ask for just a few."

2 Kings ch.4 v.3

LONDON CALLING

This is a story about a wee boy from the back streets. But not the whole story. As an unhappy child I was blissfully unaware of many things including the fact that I was unhappy. However, my world was shaken when a school mate (a smart lad) remarked that my home was "a slum." My family-safe; mum-kept-spotless; worked-hard-at-being-a-caring-home, not fit for human habitation! Yes, we had house mice and 'clocks' (cockroaches). But dad was good at setting mousetraps and he enjoyed remarkable success. Dad taught me to place Guinness in a saucer and showed me how 'clocks' were lured to death by drowning! I used to imagine those bugs getting drunk before they died. Guinness is good for you? Evidently not if you're a 'clock'!

Tiger's Bay (a.k.a. the slums) was a stone's throw from the docks and lay in the shadow of Cavehill. There was comm-unity. Neighbours were neighbours. I remember Jan; Mr and Mrs McAdell; Jinny Harkins; Mrs Creen and her daughter Lisa. Lisa was disabled in some way. She had the warmest smile. I liked Lisa and I think she liked me. There were the Elliotts; the Jordans and the McWilliams. We were neighbours and friends long before the TV shows…and before soc-I-ety.

Solomon, a black boy (the same age as me but much more mature), lived with Jan during school holidays. He called her "Aunt." During term times Solomon lived in a Children's Home. Dad's uncle Fred from Winnipeg was visiting our family. Fred couldn't believe how a white boy and a black boy could play together. Uncle Fred (I liked to call him 'uncle' as I thought this would please him) gave Solomon and me 50 pence each. This was a generous act (and on subsequent reflection a judicious one). Fair's fair whether you're black or white.

Just the other day Solomon contacted me on Facebook. I cried. My boyhood friend alive and well and happily married with a family of his own!

Let me tell you a secret: Solomon used to tell other Tiger's Bay boys that his daddy was a Nigerian businessman who, because of job commitments, had gone back to Africa. Little did I know that I was keeping up a front myself as I listened to Solomon build defences in order to protect himself.

As a frightened child I often played with infants in Ship Street (that is, when Solomon was in care). Maggie Burney commented on my behaviour, that is, the fact that I played with toddlers instead of my peers. I couldn't understand how she could discern such a thing. Her powers of observation made me feel uneasy. She 'got under my radar'. Alarm bells did ring faintly within me but my behaviour remained unchanged.

When 'our Troubles' broke out in '69, (the Summer of love!) the Burney family moved to Fairviewtown. They settled in a newly built housing estate there. It was to become a Protestant ghetto where houses had gardens and bathrooms and indoor loos. (My uncle Davy used to say; "You can take the people out of the slums but you can't take the slums out of the people"). I spent a summer on holiday with "the Burneys". Robins, chaffinches, blackbirds and seagulls were welcome attractions.

Tiger's Bay had pigeons. Some 'homing pigeons' but mostly street pigeons. The occasional 'fan-tail' was a sight for sore eyes (a sort of peacock in the pigeon world!) Once I laid a snare with thread, complete with noose and pigeon corn. Whilst crouched in the hallway of slum-home I held one end of the thread in my hand. The remainder of the thread stretched almost invisibly across the footpath, down the cribbie (the kerb) and out into the centre of the street. To my utmost surprise an unsuspecting pigeon made its way inside the noose. Immediately I pulled the thread. The noose tightened on the pigeon's feet. Instantly the bird flew up into the air like a kite on a string. As this living creature tugged hard, weighty and fighting for freedom, I felt nauseated. I hadn't the courage to pull my quarry to the ground. I let go of the thread and the pigeon flew away, its feet tethered and entangled. (I still think of that poor bird. I hope it didn't die because of my actions. Did the thread rot over time? Might the pigeon have pecked off its fetters?)

At some point Solomon stopped coming to Jan's house. You know that "the Burneys" also left 'the Bay'. But not before Eva McWilliams put James Burney's head up her jumper. Eva didn't wear a bra and James got an education. You should have seen his face light up! But he didn't tell me what he'd seen.

Barricades, bombs and bullets became the back-drop. My younger sister and I slept in bunk beds in 'the back room' (so-called because it was the smaller bedroom of two and was situated at the back of the 2-up-2-down house). My sister slept in the top bunk. As a bed-wetter I slept in the bottom bunk. At night we would lie in bed listening to the riots, the sounds of gun-fire and the piercing yells, "They've shot 'em. The bastards have shot 'em." Men in Balaclavas gave orders for disorder.

Dad provided me with a torch. At night I could use the 'potty' on the landing at the top of the stairs. If I needed to defaecate I had to go outside to the toilet in the yard. Dad had surrounded the old toilet with wood. This made for comfy sitting! But rust on the high cistern fell off like orange dandruff on one's shoulders when the chain was pulled. My slum-family were perhaps a little swanky after all. We had soft toilet roll. At Granny's, cut up squares of the 'Belfast Telegraph' hung on a loop of coarse cord which in turn hung from a nail in the toilet wall.

You might like to know that Mr McAdell was our local 'windy cleaner'. He earned his living by cleaning windows (unchallenged!) Paramilitaries didn't have a vice-like grip on working practices as yet. A man could earn a living selling ice-cream; delivering newspapers; collecting 'regs' (rags); selling vegetables from a hand-cart and didn't have to pay 'protection' or forfeit his livelihood.

Having passed the 11 plus exam I was awarded a place at the Belfast Royal Academy (a local grammar school). From the first day of term one at BRA I felt I'd made a monstrous mistake. Many kids had posh accents and their mums and dads drove fancy cars. There was even a pupils' car park! I felt inferior. My mum and Granny (my mum's mum) walked with me near to my new school. They left me on the Antrim Road. They did not accompany me to the school grounds. Did they feel as I did? At the end of the first half-day's attendance I thought to myself, "What the hell have I done?" But I had learned not to 'let on' (that is, I hid my thoughts and feelings). I had already learned to hide most matters. I had learned to hide most things that matter.

Some years after my Granny died mum told me that Granny had been illiterate. In Granny's younger days she had attended school five mornings per week. In the afternoons she and her friends would walk bare-foot and arm in arm, singing together as they went to work in the mill. Granny eventually graduated as the local midwife in her comm-unity without certifi-cate, diploma or degree. My mum once showed me the scullery (kitchen) step at Granny's slum-home. The step was slightly curved where Granny had often sharp-ened her knife (which she used when delivering babies). Granny's services were also called upon when a neigh-bour died. She 'prepared' the body. (I wasn't told what this involved. I never asked). Also I never asked, "Where do babies come from?" One big fella in the Bay said that a man had sex with a woman by climbing on her back. I thought of piggyback races and felt confused.

In Tiger's Bay the tough lads fought each other to determine the pecking order. And local men argued about which streets comprised the real Tiger's Bay. As a young resident I considered the Bay area to be bordered by Duncairn Gardens; North Queen Street; Limestone Road and Halliday's Road. My world was large and flat. Rather, an island in the midst of dangers.

As a boy I loved the fact that my mum had been able to buy me baseball boots and a parka at reduced prices. One day at BRA a group of the good-looking boys (who got the girls) were taking great delight in discussing whose shoes were the most expensive. Boy was I a fish out of water! I pretended to myself that dad (who worked as a labourer) probably spent a greater percentage of his wages on his family in proportion to that which wealthier parents spent on their kids. (I was on the defensive and kidding myself).

In the playground at Grammar school physical fights were virtually non-existent. In the classroom academic rivalry was intense. I felt stupid (and God forbid that anyone should find out). Robin, a good friend, called me a swot. He knew I regurgitated information. I didn't know. I couldn't understand what he was talking about. And he had difficulty understanding what I was talking about.

Many wonderful weekends were spent with Robin in a nice residential area on the other side of town. Robin lived in a mansion (or so it seemed to me). Even the feathered visitors were posh – quite unlike the drab pigeons in the Bay. But there was no Lisa and no 'Buck-a-boo' Tommy in the well-to-do streets (sorry, avenue; park; court; rise; manor).

Should I tell you about 'Buck-a-boo' Tommy? Well you see, the rumour in the Bay was that Tommy had had his tongue cut out by the Japanese during World War 2. When we shouted at him, "Buck-a-boo, Tommy" he would give chase. It was great fun! Probably because he never caught us! Later it was suggested to me that the poor man may have been 'tongue-tied'.

Back to Robin. Robin and I had great fun together.

(In my arrogance I assumed I was helping him. Now I realise he was helping me). But I never felt relaxed at meal times whilst seated with his family at the dining table. Which knife should I use? I would carefully watch my p's and q's. (Mr Campbell the maths teacher had corrected me in front of fellow pupils...'Ma' is mum; 'windy' is window and 'Buttchers' is bootchers!) And somewhere along the line I had learned to hate my name. When others called me 'Bill' I would feel very uncomfortable. One song I couldn't bear to listen to was:

"I met him on a Sunday and my heart stood still... somebody told me that his name was Bill."

Bill and wraith became increasingly duplicitous. I stumbled on regardless, unaware of what lay ahead. (Later I was to learn from a friend that "this sort of thing begins in the home." I resented that remark for many years. Acceptance of its truth has helped bring healing).

'O' levels were easy enough. However, I couldn't work out why some school friends achieved higher grades than me. After all, we'd been given the same notes from the same teacher. Career's advice consisted of, "Leave school and join the Bank." But by sixteen years of age I was a rebel. Not a Republican or a Nationalist, but rebellious. "I'll teach the school authorities a lesson – I'll stay on and do 'A' levels just like my peers."

Revision for 'A' levels proved very difficult. I feared that poor 'A' level results would expose me as being 'thick'. I dreaded being found out. Thus, the strain of 'A' levels nearly broke me. I decided to take one year out from education (a gap year long before gap years became fashionable, but for all the wrong reasons). Many BRA pupils got good grades and made matter of fact transitions to University life. I didn't realise that the inner pressures I was experiencing were manifesting as stress. (Exams test not only the mind but also one's mettle).

I got a job in a local factory. Six months later with $600.00 and a £60.00 Freddy-Laker Sky-Train one-way ticket I set off for New York, New York. On the flight a guy named Pete chatted to me. He had been travelling in Europe, "playing organs." (A musician, I mused). On disembarkation at JFK about twelve males, (of which I was but one member) were led to Security and Customs clearance. A Security officer did not question me about money or if I had adequate insurance cover, what my plans were, etc. Security seemed very lax but I was nervous. However, once I gave my dad's cousin's address as my contact destination and the security guard saw that I was backpacking he gave me permission to enter USA.

Beyond Customs clearance Pete my musician friend was waiting for me. He suggested getting a meal. Horror! Staff at the café would not accept my Thomas Cook travellers cheques and I had no cash. Pete paid for both meals. Afterwards, he and I walked out into the Manhattan night. The roads were aflame with the yellows and reds of headlights and tail lights. The night air was alive with sounds of traffic and the smell of diesel. Pete asked me to spend the night with him. The penny dropped. Those organs! I was terrified by the darkness, the noise, the activity. Pete's proposition momentarily seemed like a good option. After a moment's reflection I turned down Pete's offer. I would take my chances in Manhattan, with a rucksack and without accommodation. Then Pete did something very kind and caring. He phoned staff at the Vanderbilt YMCA and asked if rooms were available. He then went to a New York yellow cab taxi-driver and asked him how much it would cost to take me from JFK to the YMCA. The driver said, "$15.00." Pete gave me $15.00 cash. (I hope I thanked him). Then in the back seat of that cab I realised I was not even out of the airport! (To this day I still think of Pete. Is he alive? Has he died of aids? Will I ever meet him again?)

Further 'drop-out' years followed in Guernsey in the Channel Islands. Work, booze, eat, sleep; work, booze, eat, sleep. ("I crossed the ocean for a heart of gold and I'm growin' old"). Dropped out of two University undergraduate courses; lost the woman I thought I loved (but learned I didn't love her). Also, learned a brutal but essential lesson – my actions have consequences.

Then I applied for nurse training at the Royal Victoria Hospital, Belfast. (I was 24 years of age). Two weeks after submitting my application form I was called for interview. Then the you-know-what hit the fan! I told my parents, "I'm frightened, I'm frightened, I'm really frightened." But I didn't know what I was frightened of. (I couldn't make the transition from teenager to adult in one fell swoop!) The fear was terrifying. My GP didn't know what to do. (He probably lacked training. Maybe he didn't have the right certificate, diploma or degree). Dad was working a three-shift system so I had opportunity to sleep in his bed along with him for comfort and reassurance. Eventually medical help came in the form of Dr Smyth, Consultant Psychiatrist. He arrived at the parental home and was carrying a large brown leather briefcase. His jacket collar was turned down on one side and turned up on the other side. I thought he needed to see a psychiatrist! Dr Smyth told my parents, "We've got a very ill young man here. I'm taking him in to hospital." My mother objected but Dr Smyth replied, "He either comes in voluntarily or I have the power to take him in." Someone agreed that I would be a voluntary patient although I have no recollection as to who made that decision. I don't think it was me! I was broken but sadly my 'bluffing' had not ceased. All the 'running away', all the avoidance behaviour, culminated in an admission to Errington Psychiatric Hospital (a massive site on the outskirts of Belfast with a massive stigma to boot).

A bag was packed for me. A family friend took me in his car to Errington. I was officially mentally ill. The diagnosis was 'clinical depression'. (There is a spatial element accompanying mental illness. The ward was like a Tardis - small from the outside and large inside. As I began to feel well the 'Tardis effect' altered to a normal perspective. I'm tempted to say that Dr Who was looking after me! In fact, it was Dr Leon).

We patients were a bunch of all sorts. A six feet four ex-police officer (in his 80's) feared that the Provos would kill him. A thief was robbing the cop. A dried out alcoholic threatened to hit the thief if he didn't stop demanding money from the old policeman. Sean, with whom I later shared a side-room, didn't like to "waste an erection." A medical doctor who had been 'struck off' had to bear his wife's anger while she ranted about divorce proceedings during her visits to him. And one elderly lady continually strayed in to the men's ward. All she ever shouted was, "I want to die." There were other patients too but I think you get the picture. (Did you know that the phrase 'around the bend' originates from the fact that the Authorities built Mental Hospitals beyond City boundaries, 'around the bend of the road'. Out of sight, out of mind!)

I should have said that on arrival at hospital I was escorted to a bed next to the Nurses' station for close observation (that is, before I was considered well enough to be trusted in a side room). A young female nurse said, "Take off your clothes, put on your pyjamas and place your clothes in this bin bag." It was noon. I didn't want to be in my pyjamas at lunch time. I felt humiliated and defeated. Besides, if I had met this nurse at a disco just a few weeks earlier I might have asked her for a date! (If the truth be known I had always been 'defeated' in relationships. I had rarely 'fought back' in any situation and I certainly never had dared to ask a girl for a date at a disco!)

The first lunch time was mostly a blur. Later, fellow patients explained, "They've taken your clothes away and left you in your pyjamas so that if you run away from hospital the police can locate you more easily!" Wasn't it true that the nurse had *told* me what to do? She had not *asked* me to take off my clothes. She had not explained why she was removing the bag which contained my clothing. I was beginning to learn who my friends were and who the enemy was in this place.

It was apparent that the Consultants ruled the roost. Nurses were 'eyes and ears' for the Consultants. And patients hated being spied on. However, I could hardly wait to be placed on the Consultant's couch and for him to swing his gold pocket watch back and forth ("are you getting sleepy?") whilst I would spill out all my problems and become well. What a shock to find out this wasn't going to happen! Psychiatry is not psychotherapy or hypnosis. Besides, I didn't know what my problems were. The least I could do was blame staff for my problems!

Whilst in hospital, Simon from Andersonstown, West Belfast and Bill from Ballysillan, North Belfast (my family moved away from Tiger's Bay in 1970) became lifelong friends. Friends for 34 years until Simon's recent 'passing'. Politics and religion never marred our friendship. We had suffered too much to let Northern Ireland spoil our care and concern for one another. Alex, who loved making models and was 'bi-polar' made up the trio.

During this period (forgive me, I'm a bit hazy about dates and times) I was under the care of a young trainee GP who, if I remember correctly, was on a six months placement. He meant well and dutifully reported that I was overcome by seeing so many leaves on trees (actual trees and actual leaves!) and that I'd said there was too much print on a newspaper for me to be able to read one. He earnestly suggested that in future I should cease reading Spike Milligan books! (On reflection he had a point).

One day the trainee GP said to me, "Dr Leon wants you to have ECT." "Yes," I replied. The scene was set. The deal was done. My consent was given. I didn't know what ECT was. And I didn't know I was a people-pleaser. (In case you don't know, ECT stands for electro-convulsive therapy; better known as 'shock treatment'). ECT was administered for my deep-seated depression. This depression had weighed me down in chains and I was not Houdini. I received seven shocks (roughly two per week) and was miraculously lifted out of de-pression and put back on my feet. A phased discharge from hospital care began and then I attended a local Psychiatric Day Hospital (hospital by day and home each evening and at weekends). Then I returned to my job in the Civil Service. (At some point I had gone from being on the dole to working in a dole office).

I was deeply unhappy. Therefore, I resigned my post and enrolled as a student at Queen's University Belfast, studying for a Bachelor of Divinity degree. (More running away!) After two years of study I flunked out of College (but was still taking my medication faithfully). Then readmission to Errington Hospital. This admis-sion was more painful than the first one as I realised my problems had not gone away. I spent four months in hospital and received sixteen shocks of ECT.

In the mid '80's the process of giving ECT was like 'factory farming'. Twice per week (on ECT days) eight to ten patients (naked except for paper gown coverings) lay on trolleys. Each patient in turn was wheeled in to the room where shock treatment was given. When my turn came, an unpleasant hard reddish-brown bung was rudely placed between my teeth. I clenched hard and feared what would happen next. Anaesthetic was given and I battled to watch the second hand move on the clock on a wall. On wakening I found myself lying on the same trolley as before and in an area designated for recovery. Staff served tea and toast and shortly I was back on the ward amongst fellow patients. (In spite of the impersonal nature of the ECT procedure back then I would still advocate for a wise and limited use of such treatment. ECT delivered me from thoughts of suicide – thoughts I might otherwise have acted upon).

My illness bore down heavily on my parents. (Mental illness causes havoc in families when a loved one becomes mentally unwell). As an adolescent (aged twenty-four) I blamed my mum and dad for most of my problems. Staff, as you already know, were culpable too! How could well educated, successful, career-minded medics understand someone like me? Yet I liked being an 'in-stay' patient at Errington. Walking in the hospital grounds was a great way to unwind and relax. Besides, during episodes of acute illness I could not have coped with living at home. And the stress for my family would have been too great. (Community care may well be fashionable but fashions come and go).

Then spiritual enlightenment! I shall not bore you with the nature of the hallucination. Needless to say, it fooled me but not Dr O'Toole (my new Psychiatrist). Sadly, I became a 'religious nutter'. (You can fool some of the people some of the time but you can't fool all of the people all of the time). My diagnosis changed from that of clinical depression to schizo-affective disorder (a psychotic condition). 'Schizo' refers to schizophrenic traits; 'affective' means a tendency to mood swings, that is, elation/depression; 'disorder' speaks for itself! I still have occasional sensations when the nails of my big toes feel as though they are being twisted back. At such times no-one is physically touching me. In the past I had sensations in which my body seemed to be twisted by 'unseen forces' while I lay in bed. Descents in to what seemed like hell were persistent and with no end in sight. (In the dungeon did Joseph know if he'd ever be released? I think not, but I believe he hoped and prayed).

I ran with enlightenment (so-called) for a number of years. But I was still running away from reality. One day a doubt occurred: 'If your experience is real why is there no change in your thoughts, feelings and behaviour'? Doubts, rather this recurring doubt, troubled me increasingly. Eventually I realised that my enlightenment had been nothing more than a manifestation of profound and enduring psychiatric illness. In fact, I had suffered a powerful visual hallucination. (Mental illness is a tyrant. Of course, tyrants have their day. But tyrants can be overcome. It pays to stop and think! Never forget this my friend).

A further experience and a discovery! Some nursery rhymes have meaning!

An aside: I'd once asked my dad, "Daddy, show me the way to live." Dad replied honestly, "Son, I can't do that." Years previous a friend called Jean had stuck a dagger in my heart when she told me, "You're never happy." The truth hurts. Boy, does the truth hurt. Could this be why most people don't like the truth?

Now this unhappy boy realised he was unhappy. I had 'lost my marbles'. (I think I have earned the right to speak in such a manner!) I had been a lost soul who had lost any vestige of dignity I might otherwise have had. I still take psychiatric medication but stigma is no longer such a bitter pill to swallow.

What I have not told you is that back in 1983, after my first few days in hospital, I vowed that should I become well I would try to help other people. As a teenager I had adopted the lyric: "Light all the candles in dark dreary minds." God-like, or what! In time my search for reality would bring even greater pain. You see, this story is not only my story but a Northern Ireland story and an International one. It has an ending before a beginning. Real life is always thus patterned. I once told a sympathetic nurse that I wanted simply to be myself. The nurse calmly replied, "That's the hardest journey." Another friend put matters in a different way; "A chain is only as strong as its weakest link" and at another time said, "It takes a live fish to swim upstream." (Listening means doing).

Postscript: My mother died in 2015. She never lived long enough to see her eldest child gain better mental health and have a corresponding reduction in the need for anti-psychotic medication. I've been in my current job as a Mental Health Support Worker for the past sixteen years (full-time, permanent, paid employment). Yet it hasn't all been plain sailing. You see, medication and insight are essential. It seems to me that medication deals with symptoms but insight deals with causes. (We are fearfully and wonderfully made).

What about the wee boy from the back streets? He now lives in a semi-detached house complete with gardens, a bathroom and an indoor loo! Luxury, but not essential. And what has he learned? Mental illness knows no borders and crosses all divides. Mental illness can affect anyone, anytime, anywhere. But there is hope. You see, where there's a pain there's a problem. Where there's a problem there's a solution. And where there is a solution 'tis my responsibility to seek the answer. Right questions provide right answers. I also believe that people who are mentally ill can become agents for change in our communities, whether well or in 'recovery'.

There are two sides to every story. And everyone has at least one story to tell. I've shared a little of mine. Will you share yours? A story with a history and a future – an end and a beginning?

47902978R00018

Printed in Poland
by Amazon Fulfillment
Poland Sp. z o.o., Wrocław